Not Lost in Space But Still in a Lot of Trouble

by

———

Formatted by

Gimmicky Pseudonym

Author: Pseudonym, Gimmicky

ISBN: 978-0-6481463-8-4

Dedication:

CHAPTER ONE

09

ACKNOWLEDGEMENTS

I'd like to thank Gimmicky Pseudonym for creating this book to house my writing talent

OTHER BOOKS IN THE BLANK BOOK SERIES.

The Girl in the Title

Summer Beach

Silhouette of a Man

Not Lost in Space But Still in a Lot of Trouble

Journey to a Destination

My Life So Far

Fairy Tale